Sinking Into Me: Two Kings, A Mate, & A Clutch

Book 2 of Tentacle Love

Lily Anton

ISBN: 9781086023039

PART I: The Joining

I was nervous.

Not any more so than I usually was when it came to heading up multi-species negotiations, but if I had known what truly awaited me after all was said and done, I probably would have been overcome with anxiety...and excitement.

As it stands now, what I am heading into isn't like any of the usual long and drawn out diplomatic discussions I've had previously.

Well, I mean, it was, but considering the real threat of inter-galactic war my planet was facing, we needed all the help we could get.

Which is why I am traveling to Ulia: a planet several light-years away from my own as I am in dire need of allies to bolster our ranks and increase our military strength.

As the pilot of my ship announces that we'll be beginning our descent through the planet's atmosphere, a look out a side portal reveals Ulia in all its glory.

It's larger, much larger than my own planet, but the colors are strikingly the same, the purple-bluish hue of it causing me to feel a sharp pang of nostalgia.

I can hear the ping notifying us of an incoming message, the sound of it muted in my ears as I continue to stare down at the planet below.

Next to me, Head Liaison Fennec has barely moved a muscle, spending the entire trip simply reading and re-reading the reports and the contracts that had already been sent over.

He has barely spoken a word to me since our departure, and I know it's because he has his concerns with the whole thing.

In what seems like no time at all, the ship plants itself solidly on the landing dock, and it is when I am beginning to leave my seat that I feel a pair of eyes on me.

It's Fennec. And he's looking at me with concern.

"Evie, when they told me that we'd be offering up resources to the Ulians, I didn't think that you would be part of this deal in order to secure what we required."

Despite my position as Ambassador, it is Fennec that was usually in the trenches, directing our initiatives.

He had never wanted the spotlight that a role like mine had, which is why I keep my mouth shut when he speaks now, even though I want to tell him that if this had been his request, I'm fairly certain I would have agreed to it.

"I know." It's all I can bring myself to say.

I don't think it was the answer he was looking for as his mouth downturns. Still, he nods at me and allows me to head to the exit door.

While dresses were not practical considering the amount of traveling I do, first impressions were always important.

I had taken the opportunity before our landing to change into a long gown made of navy-blue silk, its billowy sleeves almost to the floor, and its neckline modest but leaving enough pale skin to offset how much I was fully covered.

I don't think I'm what anyone would call beautiful; not by anyone's standards I think, although I'm not ugly by any means.

I'm still young, surprising many people when they realize that I'm the Ambassador and not High Liaison Fennec who has about a decade on me.

Being in my thirties meant I still had at least ninety years to go.

My brown hair and brown eyes were quite plain to me and while I was certainly quite well-endowed in the chest area, they were more of a nuisance than a blessing and gravity had not been kind to them.

I have seen what Ulian women look like via information provided to me pre-trip...wispy and beautiful the way a willow tree was, and it has been challenging not to think of myself as an ugly tree stump in comparison.

Granted, looks aren't everything, and I know I am smart, resourceful, and have a position to match that.

Still, it was only natural to feel self-conscious sometimes. Right?

The goal of my dress, which catches the light in all sorts of ways for a striking effect, is not just for our hosts, but for the rest of my entourage.

I need to look in control and in command, while not looking like I'm either.

Oh the mindfuck that is diplomacy sometimes.

I take a deep breath as the exit door descends, the ramp lowering onto the dock and revealing a crowd of people.

The sound of musical instruments immediately fills the air with what is without a doubt, a ceremonial greeting.

As my feet finally make their way onto solid ground, I am met by several Ulians. They are not an overly large race, although those around me are all well over six feet in height.

Some have hair in all sorts of cuts and colors, and others have no hair at all. Their heights seem to be consistent, along with large oval eyes that when I see blinking, show a sparkling nictitating membrane just like a reptile. Or in this case, a shark.

It's not particularly alarming and makes sense considering only forty-five percent of the planet is land.

This is actually part of the job that I love the most: meeting new races and species across galaxies, being able to see what makes us all so different and yet surprisingly the same.

Despite all the alien races I've encountered over the last five years in my stint as Ambassador, I must admit that Ulians in particular are very striking and sophisticated in appearance.

Head Liaison Fennec steps forward and to my right, as is usual protocol, just as two Ulians step forward, their clothes much more elaborate and detailed compared to the others.

They look to be around my age, which means they are probably at least a decade older than I am considering their lifespans are longer than humans.

Along with them, another steps forward, and to my surprise it is a human woman.

The human woman smiles as her eyes find mine and she bends down at the waist, her back parallel to the ground before standing up straight once more.

"Their majesties King Nilvone and King Zunrion bid you greetings and welcome to our planet, Ambassador Evelyn Tribanus. My name is Lirus Grezinus. I am to act as your linguistics and cultural liason while you are here."

I smile warmly, knowing she just as easily could have said she'd be my translator.

Holding out my hands as a method of non-verbally expressing my thanks to their majesties, they both take one each with a soft smile, their fingers tracing a faint pattern against my skin.

I gasp faintly under my breath, the faintest of shivers running through me, one that I thought I was undetectable but Fennec notices (yet doesn't comment on).

"Thank you very much for allowing us to visit Ulia and for the very warm greeting," I state, trying to sound as sincere as I truly am.

I am doing my best to ignore the physical reaction I had just experienced as I make eye contact with them both.

One set of sea-green and another set of honey-gold eyes both look down at me warmly.

It's just nerves, that's all.

I watch now as Lirus handles the translation, while I also take a moment to watch greetings exchanged between Fennec and his Ulian counterpart, a gentleman that goes by the name of Eivos.

With initial hellos out of the way, I do my best to remember the welcoming speech I had practiced.

I begin to speak, projecting my voice loudly enough so that the crowd of Ulians around us can hear me.

I express how I am looking forward to not just a mutually beneficial partnership, but a true relationship based on what I know of their customs.

As soon I am done speaking in my tongue, I watch Lirus translate for me and can't help but note the flash of sea-green and honey-gold that are directed at me before they shoot each other a look.

The usual nerves I'm so used to have multiplied by a thousand, a heavy pit of anxiety now settling in my belly as it is impossible for me to determine what their quick exchange had been about.

I know that as a human woman, I am a top choice for Ulians when it comes to those they choose for breeding purposes; namely due to our body-regulated temperatures and the presence of key enzymes that are surprisingly beneficial to Ulian egg clutches.

Almost frantically, I attempt to shove all the scientific data I had been provided (willingly or not) out of my mind, but I can't help but shiver again as I feel the two members of royalty looking at me out of the corner of their eyes.

I had also brought gifts of course, which is what Fennec is now explaining to all the Ulians gathered around us; namely foods and rare alcoholic vintages that were cherished by Ulians but not easy to come by.

It became a long, drawn out affair as each gift was handed over individually and appeared sincerely well-received by everyone who took the time to eye them over.

I take no responsibility for all the alcohol we're gifting them, and part of me actually thinks about whether the Ulians -who spend a vast majority of time in water- actually do drink, but I trust my team, and based on the reactions we're getting, we haven't missed the mark.

Finally, the whole gift exchange thing is over (well, most of it at least), and myself and Head Liaison Fennec are invited back to the royal estate for an opportunity to relax a little bit rather than just heading directly to one of the officially planned balls that are being hosted for us.

One thing I've learned during my stint as an Ambassador: everyone -regardless of species- loves an excuse to throw a party.

ΔΔΔ

Parties and nervousness aside, negotiations start the day after my arrival and almost an entire they continue on without anything to really show for it.

The Ulians are certainly very welcoming hosts and appear to be understanding of what we tell them, and while that is great and we both agree that an alliance would benefit us both, I continue to get reports at the end of each day indicating that what we truly need (raw materials and money) are still off the table.

Ulia may not be the largest or most famous planet out there, but it is one that is immediately associated with abundance. Just the type of flora and fauna that grow here are invaluable to hundreds of neighboring planets, and thus heavy profits have been made.

The planet is certainly not suffering from a lack of resources or money (unlike my own, unfortunately).

Should we manage to secure a formal alliance, not only would I get both for my planet, but the Ulians would then have access to a greater transportation network, which would mean more opportunities to trade and build further alliances with others.

It truly would be a win-win scenario, but as I officially sit in on the seventh day of negotiations along with their majesties Nilvone and Zunrion, they appear to be unmoved on their stances so far and at this point it feels like a complete stalemate.

I have only a few days left here on Ulia in which to get them to reconsider, although much of that time has already been earmarked for other high ranking Ulians that may be able to help us through non-governmental means. It wouldn't be nearly enough, but it would be something to show for this trip at least.

The fact that the...uh...other thing hasn't come up in conversation has not escaped my notice.

My poker face isn't a good one, and I'll admit that I'm finding it harder and harder to keep a neutral façade as both rulers of Ulia test my patience.

It reaches a point where I simply stand up, temper rising just enough that I know we need a break, and walk out into the gardens adjacent to where our talks are being held.

As I stand there, taking in deep breaths of cool and crisp air, I can admit that it isn't just annoyance that drove me from the meeting room.

Since meeting both rulers, the nervousness in my gut hasn't gone away and it certainly isn't helped by the fact that as I've walked through the estate every day since I'd been here, I catch other Ulians looking at me and speaking in low tones to one another.

I'm not sure why they do that considering I haven't a clue what they're saying, so it's almost funny to me that it is by those hushed tones and heads close together that I get the universal sign of 'They're talking about you!' loud and clear.

It isn't just other Ulians though; both majesties constantly look at me whenever they think I don't see them do so.

They don't downright stare in any sort of creepy way, and in fact, whenever I catch them they hastily look away.

Still, it's making me uneasy...like I'm waiting for the other shoe to drop.

The sound of footsteps has me turning abruptly and I find King Nilvone and of course, Lirus.

I watch the king smile at me before he looks to Lirus and says a long string of melodic syllables that sound lovely but that my ears cannot truly decipher.

Lirus has been an excellent translator so far and tends to stay fairly cheery regardless of whatever she is supposed to translate. So, it is surprising when she turns to me now, looking more formal than was her usual.

"King Nilvone would like to take the time now to officially request the option to Join. He promises to provide your people with what they need in exchange for this."

'The other shoe has dropped then', I think to myself, suddenly at a loss for words.

As I do my best to unglue my tongue to where it is now stuck to the roof of my mouth, it is impossible for me not to notice how King Nilvone's gaze is on me as Lirus translates.

When I can muster up enough courage to meet his gaze, my thoughts are of a clear-watered sea.

He really does have amazing eyes.

I am aware of what the king is requesting of course, and while Ulians aren't always very open in the way they express emotions, I honestly feel that I know what he is picturing just now.

Because...I was picturing it too.

Lirus apparently isn't done translating, completely oblivious to the non-verbal communication taking place between me and the king.

"While we know this isn't a complete surprise, we are uncertain as to your knowledge and understanding when it comes to matters of Ulian reproduction..." Lirus says, her sentence trailing off.

"I got the idea in terms of what would be expected," I somehow manage to say...whether to fill the awkward tension-filled silence or to save Lirus from potential embarrassment. "Would you mind confirming with him what exactly he and King Zunrion would provide?"

I give myself a mental thumbs up for sounding my professional self and unrattled by the conversation.

Perhaps Lirus was expecting me to not be as matter-of-fact about the whole thing but she recovers nicely and goes ahead and lets the king know.

I watch King Nilvone pay close attention to what Lirus tells him before I find the man motioning to me while speaking quietly in his melodic tongue.

"Should you accept, it means taking on a role as nest parent for his majesty's offspring in exchange for the terms you are requesting plus future assistance should it be required..."

I swallow nervously, realizing that the king hasn't been motioning to me but rather has extended his hand, which I can't help but stare at.

"How...I know they are eggs but-" I'm unable to finish the sentence while my hand travels to my stomach.

My half-question coupled with my own actions gives Lirus an understanding of what I'm trying to get out.

"A nest of eggs is usually three to four on average with each being no larger than the palm of your hand," she says, actually showing me her own palm.

I am aware that human babies are much larger than that and that my body is capable of handling four palm-sized eggs, but I can't help how my belly churns just thinking about having to push them out.

"The entire process from fertilization to de-nesting takes roughly twenty-one to twenty-eight days."

I blink in surprise at that.

I had expected it to be a much quicker affair. Considering my calendar was always packed, I had thought being away for a single week was going to be tough, and now it was looking like a whole month!

I mean, I trust Fennec and the others to handle things in my absence but...being by myself on a still relatively unknown planet with a nest of eggs inside me...

The logical side of me attempts to fight through my fear.

Going through with this would mean we secure the alliance we need and we can win this fucking war and save countless people and planets from bloodshed and destruction.

What did my discomfort matter in the face of such things?

I know that we are out of options, and I never held myself above others. My duty was to the people.

It is with that last thought that I shake myself loose of my fear and reach out slowly to put my hand on top of King Nilvone's, watching as he curls his long slender digits around mine.

Head Liaison Fennec will be pissed at me for okaying this and leveraging myself this way, but it's my decision.

I can only trust that Fennec will keep things running smoothly as he always does.

With my shoulders settling down and losing some of their tension now that I've made my decision, I do feel a little better.

"When do we begin?" I ask, unsure about Ulian mating or courting rituals and whether they would even apply in this instance.

All I can hope for is that the whole thing is relatively easy and non-traumatic.

King Nilvone is speaking again, his eyes never leaving me while his fingers are still wrapped around mine as Lirus interprets.

All I can tell is that the man's tone is calm and sweet and part of me feels like he thinks I'm ready to bolt at the slightest provocation and he's afraid he'll scare me off.

Something in me warms at the belief that he is showing genuine concern and caring in this moment.

"Should you not be opposed...King Nilvone would request you

come to his chambers to begin as soon as possible. King Zunrion would arrive after implantation in order to complete the fertilization process."

Oh.

Oh.

Well...shit.

I had zero idea that both of them would take part in the whole thing, although on second thought it really shouldn't have surprised me. I was simply providing the 'nest'.

It all feels like things are happening far too quickly; I thought I'd have at least some time to come to terms with the whole thing.

For some reason, my mom's voice floats inside my head, reminding me of that old saying about ripping off a band-aid. Better to do it all in one go and as quickly as possible.

Right then.

"So...just so we're clear..." I start to speak slowly, trying to ensure there aren't any other surprises, like let's say...

Lirus getting involve and it all turning into some random foursome.

"...King Nilvone will be the one to...implant them and then King Zunrion will come in afterwards to-" I can't find it in myself to finish the sentence and thankfully, Lirus gets it.

"Correct."

"Okay then...I guess...well, let's get this show on the road..."

I'm not sure if the expression can be translated effectively, but Lirus clearly conveys my acceptance of moving forward before looking back at me.

"I shall not be present during the...exchange..."

I actually find myself biting my lip to keep from laughing. Lirus is trying quite hard to word things delicately and I give her kudos for trying.

It hadn't occurred to me that on top of what was about to happen, I have no way to verbally communicate with the Ulian once she was gone.

'You've had plenty of sex where you didn't have to say a single word to each other. It never turned out too badly for you did it?' the voice in the back of my mind decides to say with a hint of smugness.

It's not wrong.

"It would be best for you to position yourself on your hands and knees during the exchange. We have learned from experience that while the eggs are not too big upon entry, it will be more pleasurable for you if your body is appropriately...uh...situated." Lirus' face had turned red despite her professional sounding advice.

I could feel my own face heating up but luckily I wasn't much of a blusher so I knew that I wasn't suffering the same fate this poor woman was.

Still, the sudden change in topic made things seem that much more real.

All I can do is nod in understanding, doing my best not to let my imagination run wild with what's about to happen despite me voluntarily agreeing to this.

Unfortunately, it doesn't quite help me get over the whole having eggs inside of me getting bigger and bigger with each passing day.

If I have to be on all fours to make this whole process easier then I was going to do it.

I know that King Nilvone has been watching me intently during this whole conversation, and he doesn't need to have Lirus translate for me to know that he obviously wants me to be okay with the whole thing and is looking for any indication that I wish to back out of this.

I'm going to be doing this willingly.

When he sees that I still wish to move forward with this, King Nilvone escorts me in a gentlemanly-like manner: his elbow crooked in order for me to slide my arm through his and allow my hand to rest on his forearm.

The feeling of warmth I get through the sleeve of my dress settles me a little.

He leads me in a roundabout way back into the estate, which reminds me that I had simply come out to the gardens for some fresh air in the middle of an already long day of negotiations.

I know Fennec will wonder where I am and I'm not exactly certain how long I will be 'indisposed' for, but I tell myself it will be fine.

We don't speak to one another, but the silence is comfortable and the walk is pleasant, even as we ascend two flights of stairs and stop in front of a large set of double doors.

The doors open automatically, and I am surprised to find the room furnished similarly to the one I'm currently staying in.

I had thought we'd actually be going to his personal room although perhaps I should have known better.

Despite Ulians being quite comfortable on land, I knew that they were even more at home in the water, and had come to find out that resting and sleep for this particular race took place in more aquatic environments when available.

Fennec had joked that it was really just an excuse for people to have hot tubs in their rooms, when we had found out.

At the moment, I am not entirely certain as to whether this is just another room that is assigned to visiting dignitaries or if its purpose is only for what we were about to do.

I'm regretting letting Lirus leave now without having peppered her with questions.

Of course, I can always ask her after the deed is done.

I head inside the chambers as I follow King Nilvone and immediately register the soft smell of something floating in the air around us.

My eyes find several large candles that are half my height, standing several steps from the ginormous bed that is off to the side, floor to ceiling windows across from it giving a view into the expansive gardens below.

I also notice a small nightstand that has a few things on it. Namely several pieces of what look to be a version of terry cloth, a couple of glasses, a carafe of something, and a vial containing some sort of viscous fluid.

King Nilvone gestures kindly to the bed and I find myself taking a seat at the very edge of it as if it could possibly bite me.

A glass is being filled with what's in the carafe (wine, I think) and handed to me.

I accept politely with a small smile and part of me wants to down the whole thing in one gulp. I choose instead to take small little sips, as if I can push things off until my glass is empty.

I am so fucking grateful that the king isn't looking at me like I am supposed to just get naked right here and now and bend over for him.

If he had, then I honestly think I would have chickened out.

As I continue to sip my wine, the king goes and grabs that vial of viscous fluid I had spotted when I entered the room.

I don't know exactly what I was expecting but the man lowers himself to his knees in front of me, placing the vial next to him before slowly taking my foot in his hand and removing my shoe.

It's like I'm in a trance, watching the man on his knees in front of me, taking his time to remove each of my shoes and place them together off to the side in an orderly matter.

I admit I am more than a little fascinated (and to my own surprise, turned on) as he picks up the vial and opens it, allowing some of the oily substance to pool into his cupped hand.

He brings my foot up, beginning to massage my arches.

The release of tension travels up my body, the feeling causing a small approving groan to escape my mouth.

I have zero idea if this is part of the process or if he is simply doing this for my benefit, but I find that I really don't care. It feels amazing as he takes great care to massage my feet and then travel upwards to the backs of legs, working on some knots.

Those slender fingers continue to work their magic, and somehow my wine glass is forgotten and all I can think about is how much I want those hands to travel further upwards.

Some alien races have an unbelievable sense of smell, and I can only hope Ulians do not because I can feel the slickness between my legs as I unconsciously rub my thighs together.

My eyes must have fallen shut at some point because I jolt slightly at a touch on my shoulder.

I find him looking down at me with a soft smile and can't help but mutter a soft 'thank you'.

He makes a motion with a hand which I gather means wanting me to stand and I do so, immediately feeling the juices from between my legs trickle down my thigh past the barrier that was my underwear.

His hand smoothly moves to behind my neck and I feel him slowly unclasp the first button of my dress before stopping to look down at me.

I nod, my eyes closed again as I feel my dress being slowly undone and gently lowered to the ground.

I step out from where it pools around me, and while I immediately think that I would be self-conscious, I find that I feel relaxed and not as anxious as I expected to be.

'It's the candles. There's some sort of relaxant they're releasing,' I realize after taking a deep breath.

While normally such a thing would give me immediate cause for concern, my head is still very clear and I don't feel any sort of nausea or dizziness or any other concerning symptoms so I don't freak out.

Not even as I'm being led to the bed, lying down and exposing my back to the Ulian.

I can hear the sound of my dress being picked up off the floor and realize that it's being hung up somewhere.

I smile into my pillow at the thought before I notice that whatever fear I was feeling about what I had agreed to do was gone.

My main concern in all honesty was actually having eggs inside me...growing.

Shoving the picture of that away comes easier to me than I thought it would and frankly, things so far are going surprisingly better than I had imagined.

Especially since I hadn't thought there would be anything like foreplay.

Lost in my thoughts, I barely register how the bed sinks next me as King Nilvone sits on it and starts to massage my shoulders before moving to my lower back, his fingers smoothly unhooking my bra.

The warmth of his hands coupled with how he seems to know exactly how much pressure to use is fucking amazing, and I can feel myself beginning to drift asleep.

I actually must have drifted off slightly because it takes me a moment longer than it should have to realize that a chunk of time has passed and that the king's face is close to mine; his fingers caressing one of my cheeks in such a touching manner than I forget to breathe for a second.

He says something to me, something that I obviously don't understand but the uplift in his tone at the end of it means it was undoubtedly a question.

I forget that I'm lying there practically naked, and looking into those sea-green orbs makes me smile while I find myself slowly lifting my own hand and touching his cheek, mirroring his gesture.

It might sound strange, but I am actually really touched that he is being so very attentive, and with the look in his eyes now, I know he's checking in with me, making sure that I still wish to go on.

With a smile still on my face, I nod softly, and see, with a pleasant surprise, a happy smile gracing the Ulian's face before his lips are on my cheek, placing a gentle peck there.

The next few moments find me slowly sitting up and removing my bra and underwear before laying back down face first on the bed.

Other than the usual flutter of nerves I've had with new lovers, I feel calm and surprisingly safe as I lie here naked.

I can hear clothes rustling off to my side, and I find the king slowly removing his own clothing and placing them away.

I take the time then to review what Lirus had told me, and take a few moments to position pillows underneath me for support so that I don't have to hold myself up during the whole thing.

Having my ass in the air is definitely a much more vulnerable feeling and my heart is racing now as I can hear him come behind me and climb onto the bed.

Part of me wants to actually turn to look at him and catch a glimpse of what King Nilvone is working with, but as I recall forgoing photos of Ulian anatomy, I realize I'm not that brave and it's probably better to keep myself as calm as possible.

I breath in sharply as I feel fingers slowly moving inside one of my thighs, a digit caressing over the places that I know are slick with my juices, my body wanting whatever the king behind me wishes to give.

Suddenly, I feel those fingers enter me, my body tensing at the intimate contact before I allow myself to unclench and figure out quite quickly that King Nilvone apparently knows exactly what he's doing.

The Ulian's slender fingers push further and further inside me, easily caressing my g-spot and causing my arousal to appear in full force now as I buck against his hand and moan into the pillow.

I sound disgustingly loud to my own ears and my body is shoving back against his hand of its own accord.

It has been a long time since I've had sex.

Apparently, I'm not the only one that finds this pleasurable as I can hear soft rumbling behind me that definitely sounds happy.

Almost as soon as it's started, I feel those lovely fingers withdraw from my pussy, the digits dragging across my slick inner walls as if intentionally teasing me with the loss.

I whimper at sudden emptiness before it's replaced with something else almost as swiftly.

Without needing to see it, I can feel a very large appendage between my legs.

I can tell that it's colder than his fingers, thicker too, and extremely slick.

All three of those sensations are pushing against my dripping wet hole and as much as I want it, I feel myself flinch as the Ulian cock is slowly pressing into me, the friction against my walls sinfully good.

I gasp with pleasure, the amount of arousal running through me too much to be normal and I can't figure out if it's simply because I'm that turned on or if whatever slimy coating is on his cock is making me want it.

"So good, oh my god, so good! More! I can take more..."

At this point I don't even try to control myself, moaning and whimpering and saying all sorts of things.

Despite the language barrier between us, it's clearly all the sign the king needs to know I'm enjoying this and suddenly his hands are gripping my hips and he's thrusting into me with abandon.

He clearly has balls of some kind because I can feel a hot sack slapping repeatedly against my pussy and causing lewd little squelching noises each time he pistons forward.

Based on the decidedly deep grunts I can hear from him behind me, he is enjoying this just as much as I am.

With his thick, slimy girth tunneling in and out of me, I am desperately in need of more friction and resist the overwhelming urge to reach behind me and touch him.

I grind my clit against the pillows beneath me but it's not working, and I'm getting desperate enough that I hike my ass higher in the air as he's thrusting into me and quickly reach down to rub my clit.

In a matter of seconds my hand is completely covered in a mix of our combined slick but I don't care as I move my finger around in erratic circles and cry out his name as I shudder around him, my mind flashing in that moment to what it would have felt like to have had him push those eggs into me.

"Fuck yes!"

For some reason I find the idea right at this moment of climax as being insanely hot.

Whatever slime is coating his cock is apparently dulling my sensitivity so soon after my climax now as his thrusting continues and isn't unpleasant.

I am more than happy right now to simply lay here until I feel the stirrings of arousal in me again.

Surely I couldn't?

Whatever natural slickness the king has around his cock is giving way to something else now, and I gasp as I feel him expanding inside me, his rhythmic thrusting causing more friction against my walls.

Despite how much of my own slick is inside me, he's become so thick now that it hardly matters, the slight sting of pain sharpening my steadily climbing arousal.

A sudden jerk forward has him hitting that spot deep inside me that has me seeing stars.

It dawns on me now that not only has his cock gotten thicker...it's gotten longer.

I can feel the tip of him hitting my cervix with each slam into me. He hasn't come yet, but I feel something warm and hot trickle in deep inside me like some sort of teaser.

I immediately seize with pleasure.

Whatever that was has me convulsing in all sorts of good ways and not stopping.

As I experience what is the longest orgasm of my life, I barely register King Nilvone keeping himself fully sheathed inside me, his hips no longer thrusting into me.

As the climax still runs through me, I can feel my walls pulsating around him, trying to get more and more of himself into me even though my body can't physically take any more of him.

I am wrong about that though, as the king's dick is somehow moving more and more inside me despite there being nowhere else for it to go.

Something moves inside me, and I swear to god I think it's my abdomen until I feel a very egg shaped object pushing into me before my body takes over and suctions it the rest of the way through.

My tsunami of an orgasm crashes over me and falls away just as I feel that first egg moves up my body and actually situates itself in my belly.

"Nnngg, so good! More!" I beg without shame. "Please put more eggs in me...!"

It should have horrified me but what I was experiencing just felt too fucking good.

I am acutely aware of everything now, feeling egg after egg slowly making its way inside me and settle into me.

Groaning in pleasure, I can feel something heavy in my belly and my hand immediately cups my bulging stomach, which continues to grow as more and more eggs are pushed in.

I count each egg as it is laid inside me, surprised when we get to seven.

Of fucking course I would be nesting a larger than usual batch.

Despite my belly being what it is now, it hasn't actually hit me yet that I'm technically pregnant, but I do feel filled to the brim and deliciously sore.

King Nilvone's cock begins to recede, the length of him slowly pulling out of me before he leans away and re-situates me gently over the pillows.

The pressure on my belly is not pleasant, and I vaguely wonder if I have time to rest before I'm faced with whatever the fertilization process entails.

A gentle hand on my back and some soft soothing words almost lull me to sleep right then and there before my eyes shoot open as I feel something plunge into me.

I shout in surprise, my body tensing around the sudden intrusion. Whatever it is makes me feel like I'm about to be torn apart, the pain sudden and sharp before it disappears in a flash.

Warm fluid bursts upwards through me, hot, thick, and sap like as I feel it coating everything it touches.

It relentlessly pulses into me; wave after wave being shoved into me and somehow finding its way deep into my body.

I gasp, this time with my back arching in pleasure.

The heat is all-encompassing and flows quickly through me, the eggs inside me now warmer than before as they are covered with the sap-like sperm and fertilized.

Despite all the Ulian seed that was just pumped into me, there is now something warm and thin sliding in.

It slowly expands and locks itself in place, not allowing any cum to leave my body.

The soft tones of Ulian being spoken to me now comes from a deeper voice, this time belonging to King Zunrion who was for a lack of a better term, currently knotting me.

I don't want to think about how being mounted like this is causing some faint stirrings of arousal in me and focus now on being helped into a better position.

King Nilvone removes the pillows from underneath me and the sudden weight of my belly coupled with the lack of support has me buckling while the other king was still firmly knotted within me.

I can't help but look down at myself as I see how stretched out I am, my body looking like I'm many months into a human pregnancy.

My breasts, already naturally large and heavy, look puffy and slightly engorged.

One of the kings manages to get me on my side, the weight of my belly thankfully gone for now while King Zunrion is pressed in close behind me, nuzzling my neck and whispering what I'm pretty sure are soft words of praise into my skin.

It takes me a moment to realize this feeling of fullness is causing me to want (again), and considering all I have just been through, I do not waste time feeling embarrassed about moving a hand to rub my clit.

The feeling is good...almost too good, as my walls automatically clench around the thick cock still locked inside me.

I'm already close, and desperation drives me to rut back against King Zunrion.

A sob escapes me the moment I feel a slender finger come around from behind me and rub my slick pearl in my stead.

It doesn't stop me from rutting into the Ulian, and the king appears just as eager: jerking into me as much as he can while still being locked in place.

This time my orgasm is a slow wave flowing up and outwards and I groan in delight while my arm moves behind me and finds the back of the king's neck, holding him close.

As I ride out what feels like my hundredth orgasm of the day, there's another deep spurt of hot fluid pulsing into me as I quickly drift off to sleep.

PART II: The Right

When I wake up, it honestly feels like I've been hit by a freight ship after having eaten way too much food.

I also feel all snuggled up and very relaxed, which is making it difficult for me to even want to get up.

The kings are nowhere in sight, and I recognize that I'm somehow back in my original guest room and that I have on some sort of long silky black nightgown.

I have no idea how much time has passed but a look out the window shows its still daylight so it can't have been too long.

It takes me a moment to figure out what had woken me up as I hear knocking on the door which is getting more and more insistent.

With a huff, I roll myself to the side of the bed and slowly stand, wobbling a little at my sudden change in equilibrium.

My hand instinctively moves to hold my belly; an action that has me pausing in surprise as I look down.

“Fuck. I’m so full.” I whisper to myself before the knocking at the door becomes more frantic.
The ends of my nightgown swish across the marble floor as I walk over to the source of the disturbance.

“Evelyn are you in there? I swear if you don’t let me in I will smash through it.”

It’s High Liaison Fennec and he’s not using my nickname.

That’s never a good sign and I know he really would smash through.

With a sigh I open the door.

“Everything okay there?” I ask him before he’s moving me back and coming into the room, closing the door behind him.

“It's been almost twenty-four hours since I've seen you. What have you done?” he asks me sharply, looking down at me as his eyes scan over me before they freeze on my hand is resting on my noticeably large belly.

I see the blood practically drain from his face and he looks like he’s about to faint.

“You...” his frustration and ire are gone and is replaced with concern. “What did y-“

Ignoring my own surprise at how much time has passed, I do my best to shift into a more authoritative posture, which is difficult to do as I stand there pregnant and barefoot, and my hair a wild mess.

I know without being in front of a mirror that I look I've just had a thorough fucking.

"What had to be done" I answer his question before he can finish asking it. "We're getting what we came for and more."

Fennec looks at me sadly and sighs, rubbing his forehead. "I would never expect you to-"

"It was my decision. And before you ask: No, I was not forced at any point into anything without my consent."

I know he has a million questions he wants to ask me, and frankly, I don't know what he must think of me now, but there's nothing that can be done.

"Do you want me to stay or for me to get someone else to stay on Ulia with you during..." he isn't sure what to call it but gestures in circular motions to all of me.

I smile at him, honestly surprised he would offer, but I know I cannot accept that.

"No. Thank you, Fennec. The rest of you are needed. I know things will fucking fall apart if you're not there to see things through. I can handle the next three to four weeks."

"That long?" Fennec asks, eyebrows raised in surprise as his gaze flicks down to my large belly.

"Better than nine months" I counter with a smirk, watching with a smile now as he chuckles.
"True," he admits.

I place a hand on his arm, doing my best to reassure him.

"I know they will take good care of me and you can tell everyone back at headquarters that I've extended my stay to strengthen our relationship with Ulia."

Fennec narrows his eyes at me, doing a good job of assessing whether I'm being sincere.

"Should you decide otherwise at any point, you will contact me," he can't help but scold, pointing a figure at me.

I open my mouth to say something but another knock stops me and Fennec goes to answer and steps aside so that I may see who it is.

It's Lirus.

She smiles at me while a tray rests in her hands, a cup of water and a covered plate.

"Hello Ambassador Tribanus," she says pleasantly before turning to address Fennec. "High Liaison Fennec."

She focuses back on me now and moves to put the tray on the table by the window.

"I bring food for you," she states, lifting the lid off the container.

It looks like a light broth of some kind, with vegetables floating in it. I can see the steam rising up and curling as it floats into the air. Lirus begins setting a place at the table for me.

"It should be light enough not to cause you discomfort while providing you with needed nourishment. Meals like this would be best for the duration of your nesting. The kings have decreed that anything you need will be provided. I promise that you will be well taken care of while you are here."

My belly chooses that moment to grumble at the sight of food and so I sit down and get ready to eat.

I look up at Fennec before taking my first sip of broth.

"I'm fine" he insists. "I ate with Nilvone and Zunrion. It's how I knew about the sudden change in negotiations with the Ulians."

"I notice no mention of their status," I tease, wondering if he was intentionally calling them by name because he was upset.

"They insisted actually. Said that there was no longer that need for formality."

I cough slightly as I had just taken the first spoonful of broth to my lips.

That surprises me but I say nothing as I realize just how hungry I am.

As I steadily fill myself up with broth and take small bites of some fresh bread that has been placed on the side, Lirus speaks up again.

"The kings request that you meet with their chief doctor in order to confirm that the eggs are viable and that your individual physiology is allowing for a stable environment."

That brings me up short and I level Lirus with a look that has her holding up her hands in a reassuring gesture.

"Occasionally the nesting parent is unable to nest the eggs for a variety of reasons, and if that is the case then the batch is removed. It is a sad occasion should that happen but the risk of a nesting parent being in any type of danger or discomfort is not allowed."

The more Lirus speaks, the more I can see Fennec relaxing, and to be honest, I do too; feeling myself settle more.

What she's saying is reassuring because the topic of what could arise should I be unable to be a successful nest parent (for whatever the reason) had been a concern.

I worried that despite the tender affection I had been shown during the process so far, that I would simply be looked at as a host.

Also, I wasn't sure if our agreement with the Ulians was based on the health of the eggs themselves.

Lirus is more perceptive than I realize because the next words out of her mouth directly address this.

"Should the nesting not bear fruit, the kings will not renege on their pact with you or your people. The mere fact that you agreed to nest the batch was what made the terms of the agreement and not the birthing."

"Thank you" Fennec says to her.

Perhaps I've eaten too quickly because I feel a twinge in my belly and rub it gently before it settles.

Lirus is looking back at me now and seems to be choosing her words carefully.

"I wanted to provide you with some reassurance as I know you most likely are very anxious moving forward. I know that there are those who believe that becoming a nesting parent is simply a job with no emotional attachment but that is not true..."

She had my attention now as that is exactly what I had thought.

"Ambassador Tribanus, you are considered a part of the family unit, hence the term nesting parent.

What you carry inside depend on you for their development and are affected by your health and happiness and will take a part of who you are as they are molded. When they are hatched, they will be just as much yours as both King Nilvone and Zunrion's.

They will be your offspring as well should you wish it. You must know your worth."

I'm not going to lie. I am completely floored by the statement and this information is a lot to process and I honestly can't interpret all the emotions whirling around within me.
I think a small part of me actually feels humbled and before I know it I'm rubbing my belly affectionately.

It's probably a maternal instinct thing that I choose not to dwell on.

I hear Fennec taking a seat beside me. "Considering your whole family is very much aware of how much you had no desire to ever be pregnant or have kids, I guess they'll have some grandkids now, Evie."

Perhaps it's the stress of everything, but I laugh a little more than I probably should have. "Right, I'll make sure to have the kings send us photos of them."

I was trying to be funny but Lirus clearly believes I'm being serious and nods.

"I'm certain that both their majesties would be more than willing to share their development with you. You are now recognized as a member of Ulian royalty and should you bond with another and have additional offspring, they will be treated that way as well."

Wow. Okay. That was...a lot.

Apparently in the span of a single day I have gone from simply being a diplomat to being filled with eggs that I would technically have parental rights over should I wish them, and then being told I'm now somehow a member of Ulian royalty.

I need a second (or three) to get my feelings on the matter to calm down although my eyes are burning in their desire to shed tears.

It must be hormones or something.

I feel Fennec put a hand on my arm and I squeeze it gently in thanks before I turn to Lirus and hope to god my voice doesn't crack.

"I appreciate you letting me know this."

Lirus bows her head slightly and I begin to think about how this other human woman in front of me may know more about this entire thing from something other than objective facts.

I really do wish to bring it up, my curious nature wanting to know more, but it seems too personal to ask so I try to get the conversation back on track.

"Have the kings said when exactly they wish for me to meet with their doctor?"

"They recommend within a couple of days as they recognize that you may be in discomfort and would like some time to adjust," Lirus states, gently squeezing my arm in a way that seems unlike her.

Maybe I still looked like I needed reassurance.

"The chief doctor can bring what he needs to you; I believe it will be much more comfortable and much faster to have the examination done in the estate's medwing."

Considering how difficult it had been for me to walk to the door to let Fennec in, I am well aware that a trek throughout the vast estate was probably not going to happen if I needed to travel on my own two feet.

"Uh...walking is a bit challenging right now," I admit. "Would it be possible to have a personal transport seat brought to me? I'm guessing probably tomorrow or the day after when I get more used to...the changes."

Lirus nods in the affirmative. "I will have it brought to your room tomorrow and will set up the time with the doctor."

After a quick round of goodbyes, Lirus takes her leave and it is just me and Fennec.

He sighs again, looking me over once more and I actually see him smile at me.

"Please keep me updated with how you're progressing. It does sound like they are going to bend over backwards to make this as easy for you as possible."

"I will. I swear."

ΔΔΔ

Almost forty-eight hours later, Lirus is back in my room and helping me head to my doctor's appointment.

Fennec has taken his leave; something I had forced him to do because the longer he stayed the harder it would be to see him go.

He ensured everyone knew exactly how to contact him and that he expected regular updates or he'd raise hell.

I think everyone believed him.

Even though I have had a couple of days to adjust to how heavy I am, it is still a bit disorienting and I'm still finding it difficult to stay standing for more than ten minutes at a time.

I am getting more and more concerned that things are only going to get worse from here and that I'll find myself pregnant and bedridden for the next twenty-some days.

Lirus keeps insisting that this is all par for the course and that in a few more days I will be feel much better despite the fact that the eggs are no doubt already growing inside me.

The doctor is a pleasant sounding Ulian by the name of Rinkon, and even though I cannot understand what he's saying, his bedside manner is a good one.

That helps because the examination is obviously of an intimate kind and he's thankfully telling me via Lirus what he's doing before he actually does it.

Basically he's checking to see if the entire clutch is fertilized and that there hasn't been any adverse effects of them being in my body.

The whole thing still feels weird and sudden and makes me wonder if the nine months gestation for humans is to allow the mother to mentally prepare herself.

Not only am I only going to be pregnant for about a month, but the fullness I was feeling wasn't just from my belly.

Rinkon explains that for lack of a better term, a mucus plug, was wedged inside my entrance, in order to ensure King Zunrion's seed was fully absorbed by my body.

The thought of the king's knot, coupled with the fact that he had left something inside of me now, ensuring I was bred good and proper has me heating up.

I desperately need this examination over with so I can masturbate.

The doctor and Lirus don't have a clue that I'm aroused as fuck and I know that if it weren't for that plug inside me I would probably be soaking through my medical gown and into the bench I'm lying on.

Rinkon chooses this moment to let me know that the plug is already beginning to dissolve and should be fully gone by the end of the week.

My desperate need to come aside, I am a bit baffled as to why neither king has been present for the appointment and that I have not seen either of them since our 'joining'.

I remember Lirus' statements about how this wasn't supposed to be an emotionless role but I can't help but feel like I am simply playing alien baby host.

I can only assume that Lirus is here on their behalf and will most likely let them know how the examination goes.

Another thing that has changed over the last couple of days is that I have been moved to another room; this one much bigger and grander and apparently very much near the kings' own.

Thankfully the examination is concluded fairly quickly and test results come back in a matter of minutes, the Ulian doctor smiling softly at me.

I get the all clear as well as several yoga-type poses and activities to keep me relaxed and comfortable, as well prenatal supplements.

Lirus looks absolutely ecstatic, and I hold back a joke about asking her whether or not she's actually the one pregnant.

"I must return to the kings immediately and let them know the great news. You must prepare yourself now as no doubt they will hold a grand celebratory dinner this evening in light of this!"

Without another word, she scurries off, leaving me with the

Rinkon who I shrug at and he chuckles in response.

ΔΔΔ

Sure enough, that evening the kings host a very large banquet that is so much more elaborate than the initial ones that had been thrown for me and my team upon our arrival.
I swear I think that the whole population of Ulia is in attendance and there's hundreds of different types of things to nibble on and drink that I so very much want to try but have been gently warned not to do so.

Right.

Pregnant.

I have needed to remind myself a few times already this evening.

For the first time in days, I actually see both King Nilvone and King Zunrion as I am led to a chair that is situated between the two of them as we go to sit down for main courses.

I am a little uncomfortable at first, seeing as how the last time they saw me I was naked and begging for it, but they both smile at me; King Nilvone standing up to bring my seat back while King Zunrion is escorting me by the hand to be seated.

Lirus herself is seated a few spaces away from me but thankfully translation isn't required as their majesties keep gazing softly at me and my stomach (which is intentionally highlighted by my dress's bands of gold ribbon).

They are both extremely respectful, gesturing towards my stomach in a polite manner as they request the opportunity to feel for themselves what is growing inside me.

I, of course, allow them to do so, and the rest of dinner is spent with the two kings having moved their seats closer to me.

I pretend not to notice and refuse to let a rush of delight affect me.

Once dinner is over, I am escorted to the great hall in which three large chairs have been placed on a raised platform.

Surprisingly, I am led to the largest chair in the middle, with both kings taking the seats on either side of me.

It is unexpected and makes me nervous, especially as I watch so many people begin to fill the vast hall and look up at us.

The Ulians are a big fan of gift giving and receiving, and so I shouldn't have been surprised that for the next two hours I have hundreds of Ulians coming forward and offering us presents of all sorts.

I find the whole thing extremely interesting as some of the presents are sacred texts or well-crafted Ulian good-luck charms meant to offer us health and happiness and give me a better understanding of Ulian culture and traditions.

Other presents are more pragmatic, with different tonics and herbs as well as some delightfully sweet Ulian treats that I have been given the OK to actually eat.

I am so grateful and humbled by all the gifts, but the large box of treats is up there on the list.

Lirus is sitting nearby, and I turn to ask her how to properly convey my thanks in Ulian.

At first she says it for me, and I shake my head, asking her to repeat the words slowly so I can do my best to mirror them as I look at the Ulian noble that had presented me with the Ulian confections.

My effort to speak Ulian has the kings exchanging surprised glances that I don't see, and I am surprised that my garbled Ulian visibly affects the noble in front me.

The man immediately kneels in front of me, a fist touching his chest in a sign of respect before he stands up and requests my hand which he brings up to his forehead.

Lirus gasps beside me but when I look to her she is grinning so wide I think I might have broken her.

"You do him a great honor, Evelyn."

At least I had been able to get Lirus to start calling me by my name.

I mean, considering she had explained Ulian sex acts and had been with me during a gyno visit, it only made sense that we be on a first name basis.

Clearly she was getting more comfortable around me.

I had no idea that my attempt at an Ulian thank you would be met with such a reaction, but I can hear Ulians around us speaking excitedly to each other now.

Apparently they approve of me even more.

By the time the last Ulian has presented their gift, my back is slightly stiff and I am beginning to get restless.

Not that I didn't enjoy all of this, but my body is telling me it isn't all that enthused anymore.

The evening send-off comes with a shower of colorful sparks shot into the sky, everyone oo-ing and ah-ing at the sight.

Myself included.

Despite the splendor of the evening, I can't help but feel alone now as the kings stand before me and bow to take their leave.

They each bring my hand to their foreheads and wish me goodnight, leaving me here in the gardens while Lirus is speaking animatedly with a couple of people nearby.

I decide to walk around a bit to enjoy the fresh night air, although it is difficult not to feel self-conscious as I do so.

The women are tall and slender, and it looks that I am the only one among the many in attendance that is nesting.

My dress does nothing to hide my belly, which as of this morning, has decided to stick out even further.

I hadn't thought about how all my clothes would just suddenly no longer fit me when I had agreed to this whole thing but the Ulians had been proactive, and I had swiftly found myself with a closet full of what was obviously maternity wear.

While I do enjoy wearing pants more than dresses, the dresses are simply easier to put on and are actually quite pretty if not a little bit off-putting at first.

As I walk by a large group of Ulians, they pause in their conversation to look at me with what appears to be gentle expressions, raising their hands to me in greeting.

Apparently my situation is considered a great honor, which means that every single dress that I have been provided is meant to ensure that my stomach and breasts are accentuated by well-placed stitching and embellishments.

Don't get the wrong idea; I am almost fully covered in silk, but my pregnant silhouette certainly defines it.

The way all the Ulians look at me actually makes me feel bit better, and I smile at them as I instinctively cradle my belly.

As I move on, I realize that I am completely worn out.

I let Lirus know I'm going back to my room and grab my personal transport seat to head off.

I'm too tired for a bath and the bed looks so very enticing that I simply work my way out of my dress and underwear, groaning as my breasts are now free of their cage.

They're still puffy and have taken to being slightly sore, but I gently massage them as best I can before I crawl into bed

.

I can't tell you how challenging it was to figure out the best sleep position, but I have slept well the last several nights, my body and mind too exhausted to overthink like it used to and I simply drop off to sleep in a matter of seconds.

ΔΔΔ

I wake up the next morning with a tired groan and to the sound of gentle knocking at my door.

I know who it is based on the knock and tell her to come in but warn her I'm not dressed.

Lirus appears a second later, moving into the room with her eyes averted and reaching for a robe that was hanging in the closet and handing it to me.

"I'm sorry to disturb you but you indicated to be woken up should it get too late in the day," she informs me while I slowly drag myself out of bed.

The effort to heave myself up feels like it's more than it was yesterday, and my hands are supporting the weighty underside of my belly as I finally stand and put on the robe.

"That's okay. What's up?" I ask her, tying the robe around me.

Lirus turns around with a smile, looking fondly at my stomach. It's difficult to describe but while part of me feels like a whale, the other part of me feels...satisfied.

As if this was what my body had craved.

I try not to think about the changes taking place within me or the thoughts that go along with it.

"Evie, their majesties would like to know if you would be willing to meet with them privately if you are feeling up to it today...," Lirus states.

"...They are aware that the changes you are experiencing, as well as the lack of support from your people being here may be distressing and they would like to provide you with a moment to relax and be at ease."

It must be fucking hormones or something because I can feel tears spring to my eyes and I blink them away quickly.

I hadn't realized until she had said that, how much I missed Fennec and the others.

"Do you know how much time they want with me?"

I really hope I don't sound like an asshole but honestly I find myself just wanting to go back to bed and curl up underneath the blankets for the rest of the day.

Lirus reaches over and squeezes my hand. "Not long. Most likely a couple of hours."

I move to sit down when she takes the seat opposite me.

"There is an Ulian rite of tradition that they both want you to participate in that will make you feel better. Should you not feel up for it this evening they will not take offense and will understand. It is not compulsory."

I don't know what's wrong with me exactly but there's a real risk of me crying and I don't want that.

I do my best to smile.

"It's fine. Today is good. Can you tell me about this rite of tradition?"

Lirus nods as she gets up and without prompting helps me to the bathroom and continues the conversation through the closed door.

After doing my business, I can't help but stare at myself in the mirror before my hand moves lower and I press a finger inside my entrance gently, wondering if I'll feel that plug the doctor talked about.

I do feel something thicker than usual coating my walls but my finger sinks all the way through which I take as a sign that all of King Zunrion's seed was absorbed.

I shiver at the thought at the same time as I realize Lirus is still speaking.

"The rite the kings wish to complete with you is a large part of Ulian tradition. They will slowly cleanse you in order to provide you with Ulian benedictions. The time you spend together during the process is considered extremely intimate so I am unable to be there but I will be able to answer any questions before hand."

As I'm still in the privacy of the bathroom, I allow my robe to open and watch my reflection as I rub a hand over my belly.

I have been informed that the last week will have the most sudden changes, so for now I get to go around looking like I'm in the beginning of a third trimester of a human pregnancy.

For some reason, all I can think about as I caress my stomach is the time both kings spent last night caring for me and what I carried.

Thinking of being cleansed by them is certainly appealing but having them see my body like this while not being in the throes of passion is a little daunting.

Tying my robe closed again, I leave the bathroom and begin to get dressed, letting Lirus she was fine to stay.

"What precisely happens during this time? It can't just be a group bathtime."

Lirus, whose back is towards me now, was quiet for a bit.

"There are a variety of ways that Ulians choose to perform this rite. You will be cleansed and massaged with serums but I do not know specifically which ones. It is highly pleasurable though, and while the proceedings are not meant to be erotic per se, there are many who find it to be so."

I shiver again, unsure of how to respond. Lirus misinterprets my silence.

"Their majesties will do what you give them permission to do and no more. Their intentions are not to frighten you or cause you any pain. Having been a nesting parent myself, I enjoyed the proceedings immensely. The relationship it helped develop with my loved ones made me decide to stay..."

My eyebrows almost shoot off my face as my earlier suspicions are confirmed and I let her know it's okay to turn around now.

It makes me feel so much better to know she has actually gone through this and that her previous words of reassurance and her advice have come from personal experience.

"You've done this before" I say, confirming it out loud.

"Yes. I have twice between a nesting parent."

She's done this *twice*?

"So, um..." I attempt to sound nonchalant but it doesn't really work. "You're still involved with the parents then?"

Lirus chuckles, nodding her head.

"Yes. At first it was a bit similar to your position. I was asked to help with procreation of the species and it was a mutually beneficial arrangement. But over time...it grew into great fondness and adoration. Ulians bond forever and at first I thought that was only something Ulians could experience before I was invited to join their union.

The way in which Lirus tells me this...I can hear the love and devotion she has for her partners and it sounds like the Ulians she has bonded with feel the same.

I am dying to know more of Lirus' story now but perhaps another time...

I can't help but smile for her though. "I am glad that you are happy here and have a lovely family."

I'm surprised that my statement makes her eyes water and she nods her head.

"Thank you. If you wish, perhaps when you are done with your birthing, you could meet them?

I ignore the thought of 'birthing' and simply focus on the rest of what she said.

"Yes. I would like that very much."

The rest of our time together is filled with small talk as I finish getting ready and we both walk over to the kings' room as it's a close enough trek for me to manage on foot.

Other than picking out a dress, I realize that maybe I should have actually done something about the rest of my appearance.

Fuck. I should have actually showered despite the whole 'about to cleansed' thing.

Lirus knocks on their door on my behalf as I stand there and I quickly tie my hair back into a sloppy bun so I don't look like such a mess.

The door opens although only a few inches, and Lirus speaks to one of the kings through the opening.

Apparently I am the only one allowed inside the chamber at this time which means Lirus isn't allowed to see anything more.

I can't see which of the kings it is, and Lirus concludes her conversation with the member of Ulian royalty.

"You will revel in this experience. Trust me," she says, winking at me.

That is definitely a side of Lirus I haven't seen before and it makes me like her even more.

I laugh softly now while the door in front of me opens and both kings step out together at the same time.

They smile down at me and I smile up at them and try not to think about how I feel like melting into a puddle at their feet as their eyes pleasantly scan me over as if to ensure I am well.

Lirus translates what she's saying to them.

"I presented Ambassador Tribanus with your offer and have explained what the rite entails. She has expressed her agreement in participating."

"You can tell them that Evie is fine," I can't help but interrupt. I know that Fennec had mentioned that the kings had told him to call them by their names.

Plus, it seems strange all things considered to keep on with the titles considering they have both rutted into me.

And I them.

I watch the kings exchange a glance before King Nilvone speaks.

Lirus smiles and turns to me although my eyes are glued to the sea-green gaze looking back.

"The kings would like you to also use their names. They would like to ensure that you feel you are being treated as an equal."

"Thank you...Nilvone and Zunrion."

I can tell by the way they react to me saying their names that they are extremely happy.

Both of them take a step towards me and as they extend their arms, I think that they are planning to bring my hand to their forehead again as is customary.

Instead, I feel the fingers of both my hands intertwine with theirs and in this moment it actually is like I am not some sort of third wheel.

For some reason, the gesture feels safe and welcoming and emotion threatens to overwhelm me.

Fucking hormones.

My emotions settle down but my eyes are glued to where our hands are all still together.

Zunrion is saying something as he squeezes my hand gently.

"King Zunrion would like to again ensure you desire of your own free will to participate in this rite. He does not want you to think that it has any ill consequence for you should you not, or that the offspring inside you would be negatively affected and thus nullify your agreement. It is only meant to be a special tradition in order to help you all bond."

It really should freak me the hell out but I'm not frightened and I don't think twice before shaking my head.

"I thank them both for their well-meaning insistence on making sure I want this, but I am certain."

Lirus does the last bit of translating before she makes sure I don't have any last minute questions and leaves us be.

I am led into their room now and it's just the three of us yet again.

The layout of their room is quite similar to mine but I am being walked to a side room that I had initially thought was a bathroom.

When I get there, I realize that yes, it is a bathroom, but the plunge bath is ginormous.

I don't know why I keep forgetting that they're an aquatic species.

There is a smell that instantly hits my nose that I can immediately identify as the same one from our time during the joining.

I can feel my shoulders lose some of their tension and even my back feels some relief.

I also must be having a Pavlovian response to the scent because I feel my nipples harden and a warmth settle between my legs.

So lost in thought am I that Nilvone caresses my cheek and tilts my face towards him.

He truly is beautiful.

With my focus on him now, I watch as his fingers trace the sleeves of my dress before moving to my back and tracing the invisible binding there.

I feel a gentle tug as he looks at me, the question in his eyes clear as I nod back shyly.

Both Ulians begin to slowly and methodically undress me, fingers lingering on bare skin as if to worship every bit of it they come in contact with.

It is an overwhelming feeling, especially as my bra is removed and my breasts are laid bare : large and abundant and unfortunately not as perky as I wished them to be.

The smell of those candles burning help to keep me calm even as I stand there with my pregnant and very naked body on display for them.

They lead me to the plunge bath; Zunrion by my hand, and Nilvone by touch on my lower back.

They have both already removed their own clothing while having removed mine and I'm slowly being escorted into the warm water, each step allowing me to sink further down into the hot bath.

There is a curved marble bench in the center, shaped for someone to be able to lay upon it while keeping their head well above water.

Nilvone helps me to take my place upon it, the combination of the heat and buoyancy of the water doing a great deal to help my whole body decompress.

I could almost picture myself simply getting some sort of spa treatment right now.

As I lay there, the water gently lapping against my shoulders, it is impossible for me not be in awe of the two very naked men standing above me even if water covers them from the hips down.

Both lean over me and kiss my forehead before kind fingers are brushing over my eyes and requesting me to close them.

The implicit trust I feel in this moment is truly astonishing, but I think of nothing right now except the feel of water being carefully poured over my hair and shoulders over and over again.

It's like I'm in some sort of meditative state, even though I can hear Nilvone and Zunrion conversing in hushed voices.

Despite not knowing that they are saying, I find myself tilting backwards of my own accord, somehow knowing that's what I was going to be asked to do.

Even though I cannot understand what they are saying, somehow I am figuring out the meaning behind it through whatever bond we have at this point.

I crack an eye open and find that Zunrion is pouring some sort of oily serum into his hands and I catch the scent of vanilla before fingers drag along my scalp and make my toes curl.

A hum of pleasure escapes my lips.

I am such a sucker for a good head massage and the delicious back and forth is causing lovely tingles from the base of my spine all the way to my neck.

It goes on like that for I don't know how long before Nilvone is lathering up soap and beginning to cleanse the rest of me, using the time to massage away knots in places I hadn't realized there'd been any.

My belly is also being paid particular attention to, and for some reason the touches there cause little jolts of pleasure to run through me and my moan this time is one of need.

It shocks me enough to open my eyes but it's what I feel from them...a sense of satisfaction, of pride that they have caused that reaction in me, that allows me to remain unembarrassed.

Considering the point of this is to provide me with comfort, they're doing a great job of it.

Every part of me has been cleansed now, and while I loath to leave the comfort of the water, I slowly attempt to sit up only to have tender hands pause me and have me settle back down.

Both kings are on their knees now, still tall enough for their heads to remain above water, but the sudden change in perception throws me off for a minute.

The melodic sound of Ulian being spoken is directed at me, and Zunrion, with his eyes the color of golden honey, are inches away from my own.

The proximity makes something in me twist.

He brings his forehead to rest across mine and repeats whatever it was he has just said.

I can feel heat tracing down my body between my legs and I

know that it is a direct result of what he is trying to convey.

Nodding my head, I dare to open my eyes and watch as his head slowly lowers down into the water, his lips tracing my skin as he kisses down my body and to my feet before beginning a tortuous climb up my legs and towards my inner thighs.

For a moment I find myself wondering how he's able to breathe before realizing with a small breathy laugh that it's a non-issue.

Just when I think he can't move any slower, his head is between my thighs and I feel something cool and slimy circling my clit.

I shout in surprise just has I feel fingers pushing into me with relative ease and I jerk suddenly.

His hands are on my hips, and he's driving my pussy into his face.

Zunrion's tongue is longer than it has any right to be and he's licking across my clit like he's a thirsty animal lapping up precious water.

With those beautiful fingers still inside me, I feel them curling, hitting that brilliant fucking place deep in my center and I know I'm so fucking close.

I just need a bit more and—

I keen at the sudden loss of fingers and tongue, but suddenly there's a small pinch to one of my nipples and a deliciously hot mouth that has its tongue circling a darkened pebble.

Then, he's sucking.

My breasts tingle at the sensation and my hands are scrambling for purchase; my nails digging into his shoulders underneath the water.

I feel like I'm being beautifully destroyed as I arch up into him, gasping for air.

As the pressure in my breasts intensify, I feel my thighs being held and pulled open by Nilvone.

"Fuck!" I cry out, feeling another tongue piercing my entrance and dragging across my walls, its search for my g-spot paying off.

I feel that tongue curl up inside of my cunt and I cry out, giving the men that are damn near worshiping my body a signal for more.

Target acquired, I feel Nilvone focusing his ministrations there, pushing his tongue inside me with piston-like strokes until I start to tremble.

My moaning is getting more intense until I feel a hand caress the crease of my thigh before fingers are rubbing my swollen clit.

Once...Twice...and I can hear myself shouting to the heavens as I come, *hard*.

I can feel my pussy rippling around the tongue that is still inside me and the feeling is so damn good that I never want it to stop.

It's still pushing into me, that tongue, turning this way and that way against my walls and I can't stop shaking now, sobbing through moans and trying to move away because it feels like it might be too much.

I am unable to move, and instead of being let go, I feel Nilvone's face more forcefully pushing in between my legs, a finger moving around my clit relentlessly and suddenly I can feel something rising like a torrent within me.

Oh my god.

"Fuck! I'm-I'm-" my voice escapes me as my fingers are somehow gripping his hair.

"I'm gonna come! Fuck! I'm coming!"

Despite being under water, I feel a moan of approval as a tongue keeps twirling around my swollen clit.

My heart feels like it's going to burst from my chest and all I want is to meld my body with his no matter how much I'm being held down by Zunrion.

Within seconds, everything around me stops before I'm coming again; gentle hands and mouths easing me through residual tremors.

I can't stop shaking and although no one is holding me down now, I find myself unable to move.

So here I am: naked, flushed, legs wantonly spread, nipples

swollen, and pregnant belly heaving up and down.

Nothing in my life has felt so good.

I am allowed to rest for a few minutes before I'm slowly being led out of the plunge bath and wrapped in soft cloths.

Other than the bath part, I don't know what I'm supposed to do now, but apparently that's quickly solved as they take time to dry my body and my hair before both men lead me back to the main room and onto the center of the bed.

Sleep is already fast approaching me as I slip under the heavy comforter, but not before I feel warmth surrounding me; arms encasing me while cradling my belly.

The sense of 'one-ness' I feel in this moment only serves to remind me of the love I saw in Lirus' eyes when she spoke about her Ulian family.

PART III: Nest Day

It's a week after that memorable night and I'm currently sitting and having lunch with Lirus in the outside gardens, using my stomach to rest my beverage glass on.

My belly has definitely grown, and as of this morning, I woke to the feeling of shifting masses inside me which had me concerned until I was reassured it was normal.

"If it's possible, I would like to try and learn Ulian," I tell her. "I'm aware they have a pretty solid comprehension of what I'm saying but it feels...selfish of me not to try and learn, especially since I don't expect you to constantly be here."

I don't have to tell her that I can feel the brushes of the kings emotions when they are nearby.

Lirus nods in delight.

"I can certainly plan for an instructor to come and teach you. It's actually how I picked up the language myself. Although as you're only here a short while it might not be much, but we can always plan for distance courses if you end up deciding to keep up with it."

I smile back, more than happy with that idea while my hand is resting against my belly as I feel the clutch moving about within me yet again.

It should go without saying that I absolutely want to keep in touch with Nilvone and Zunrion after the birthing.

"Great."

ΔΔΔ

As the days turn into weeks, I end up acquiring a whole lot more information about nesting parents and their final stages.

We're on Day 23 and I'm well within my birthing range.

I'm actually informed that when it is time for the eggs to leave me it is known as 'Nest Day' and that the babies will leave the safety of their eggs the same day.

Lirus and Rinkon review all the information regarding the plan of action with me.

I am told that it won't initially feel like it is pleasurable but as soon as I go properly into labor I will be taken to a Birthing Well as the water there will be laced with components that will prevent me from feeling much pain.

As soon as the last of the clutch has been birthed, I will be cleaned and helped into an Ulian Restorative Pod which will exponentially speed up my body's recovery post-birth.

I have to say, it makes me feel both good and scared to know there's a plan for it all.

When it comes to Nilvone and Zunrion, my previous concern about them not wanting to be around is completely irrelevant now.

Both of them have been a constant presence, always checking in with me and seeing how my nesting is going and whether I have any questions about what is to come.

Not only do they worry about my health, but they also check and see how I am feeling on an emotional level.

In fact, I'm hardly by myself anymore; if I'm not with Nilvone or Zunrion, then Lirus is with me or the instructor that has been helping me in learning Ulian.

I keep in touch with Fennec via Ulian's video channels and while it feels weird to stand up and hold my fully formed belly when he asks to see how I'm doing, he actually smiles at me.

"You look...happy. Glowing even," he says softly at the end of one of our conversations.

I roll my eyes but he shakes his head at me on the monitor.

"I mean it."

Not really knowing what to say to that, I jokingly tell him he just wants me to stay here so that he can take my job.

He gives me a two-finger salute that I gasp at in mock outrage before we say our goodbyes.

I try to walk as much as I possibly can every day without pushing myself.

Even with the discomfort I occasionally experience as my belly has gotten so big with the clutch, I have been extremely happy over the past twenty-some days in the home stretch to Nest Day.

Both Nilvone and Zunrion enjoy presenting me with all sorts of gifts which I've been trying to tell them I really don't need and that they don't have to go through the trouble but they don't seem to care.

The gifts keep on coming.

The 'gift' I really want is to spend intimate time with them but I'm too scared to ask Lirus if that's a thing or if that night after the cleansing rite had been a one time deal.

What I do appreciate though, is how they actually dedicate time to speak with me (Lirus and my toddler-level Ulian language skills helping me out) and genuinely wish to learn more about me.

Sometimes I am with one of them and other times I'm with both, and I learn as we spend days together that their personalities are quite different.

Nilvone is the more stoic one but prone to spontaneity, while Zunrion is more outgoing but surprisingly more pragmatic than his partner.

I can see how well their traits mesh together and I can tell that they really are a great pair.

Much of my days pass the same: with me learning more and more Ulian and staying as active as possible.

ΔΔΔ

Around two o'clock in the afternoon on Day 27 of nesting, a painful cramp shoots down my lower back, followed swiftly by another.

By this time into my pregnancy, I have only been able to stand for short periods before aches and pains make themselves known within me.

On top of that, I really do look like I've swallowed one of those beach balls that are popular on Planet Crystolos.

Considering how quickly and how painful that had just been, I'm grateful that I'm not by myself...otherwise I'm pretty sure I would have started to panic.

From Day 20, I'd been watched almost non-stop as everyone waited for my Nest Day.

As soon as the cramps run through me, I am relieved that I am in the company of Zunrion as we sit in the solarium as I am (or was, I should say) enjoying the Ulian version of tea.

I still don't feel like I know enough to communicate properly or have much of a conversation in Ulian, but I have learned enough to ask and understand simple subject matters and it's made me feel more connected to both men.

"Zunrion...it's starting..." I manage to say in Ulian, another cramp causing my back to spasm hard and making me grab for the nearest thing to squeeze which turns out to be the king's hand.

I am unable to say anything else as I grimace at the pain.

It hurts, but no where near where I think actual human labor feels like.

Still, it's not pleasant and I find myself giving women massive kudos for doing this since the dawn the civilization.

Zunrion's already large eyes look even larger as he bolts upright.

He looks like such the nervous father than I can't help but chuckle.

Luckily for me, it doesn't take him more than few seconds before he comes back to himself and scoops me up with little effort even though I know I weigh a lot.

I forget just how much strength they actually have and just how quickly they can run.

I'm placed in my personal transport seat and a moment later he's running all out down the corridor, navigating with ease while I hold on tight and hope to hell we don't crash.

My adrenaline is now going from both the ride and the onset of labor, and I try and catch my breath as I'm taken into the nesting room that happens to be adjacent to Dr. Rinkon's main office.

The cramps have stopped for now which I'm extremely thankful for as Zunrion wastes no time in helping me into the Bathing Well, the shallow water the perfect temperature.

I am fully clothed as I stand there in the water, but Zunrion efficiently helps me out of my dress and underthings, tossing them away from us.

I hear them land somewhere with a wet splat and want to laugh but another cramp runs through me, this one really fucking hurting and making me need to sit down in the water.

My position in the water helps with the cramping, but I can still feel the muscles in my stomach and back tensing and suddenly I feel a rush of liquid leave me.

Despite how much they had all gone over this whole process with me, I was beginning to panic; something that Zunrion could feel through our bond as he immediately moved to sit behind me in the water (clothes and all), massaging my stomach and offering me calm words of encouragement that I can sort of understand.

"I'm...I don't know if I can do this..."

Just as I say that, I hear the sound of frantic running and look up to see Nilvone practically screech to a halt inside, looking wide-eyed and panicked and like he would be absolutely no help whatsoever to me.

Thankfully, he's followed by Lirus, who I know is here to help translate but that I'm actually so fucking glad to see.

She has gone through this before, and if she could do it, then I can as well.

I don't really care about my nakedness right now, but Lirus is facing away from me and takes a seat off to the side; here if I need her but out of the way if not.

Rinkon finally arrives and finds both Zunrion and Nilvone now naked in the Birthing Well with me and moves to give them a large container that contains a light pink viscous substance.

I'm told that it is actually a form of medicinal lube that will not dissolve in the water and will help relax and numb my body enough so that I won't feel like I'm dying.

Yay me.

With the Ulian's big on tradition, I know what comes next as the non-nesting parents are meant to ensure I am well lubed and ready to go even if my human body is capable of birthing things much bigger than this.

Yeah. I'll take all the help I can get.

Right now, I don't feel anything really besides the tension in my belly as the clutch begin to move about, my belly changing shape as weight sinks lower and my center of gravity shifts, the water keeping the pain out of my back.

I can honestly feel eggs ordering themselves within me but I'm distracted now as both Zunrion and Nilvone insert their fingers into my pussy, attempting to loosen my walls while rubbing the lube into them.

Looking down between my legs, I see both their hands working me open and I can't help but cry out in pleasure as an orgasm tears through me out of nowhere and I frantically grab hold of their arms and ride out my climax.

"What the fuck was that..." I breathe out eventually, my back resting back against Zunrion.

I am embarrassed; something that both kings pick up on because they're immediately speaking to Rinkon before Lirus' familiar voice echoes around the room.

"It is perfectly natural and part of the birthing process. It is your body's way of making the passage of the eggs pleasurable rather than painful."

I have to give Lirus massive props for sounding so medical about it rather than embarrassed for having heard me come.

Despite the nice after-effects, there's a sudden pressure in my lower belly that is now just shy of painful and I just know that whatever was in that lube has worked fast.

I grunt in surprise, my hand now clutching my stomach and causing Rinkon to come over with a medical device and take a reading.

He says something, but it's directed at the kings.

Zunrion stays steadfastly behind me; his legs spread open to accommodate me resting between them, and Nilvone remains perched between my legs in front of me.

Whatever the doctor said has both men now rubbing my stomach in a downward motion.

It is clearly a tried and true method as I feel the eggs sink lower inside me until there's mounting pressure and suddenly I feel the need to push.

"I need to push! I need to-argh!" I cry out, the pressure almost overwhelming as I don't wait for a response and simply push as hard as I can.

I can hear Ulian words of praise being said to me and I try to believe them as I feel something inside me flex and release before an egg begins to slide out of me, the pressure inside my body gone for the moment.

There hadn't been pain but it was definitely not fun and I am already exhausted and just thinking about how many more times I have to do this is scaring the crap out of me.

I see Rinkon being handed the first egg by Nilvone and it is placed into a floating container off to the side but still in the water.

I'm not sure if I want to see it but I choose to look, my jaw hanging open as I see a beautiful pearlescent shell slightly larger than my fist.

Apparently, these were going to be bigger than what Lirus had assured me would be their size.

My break is over now as pressure builds again and feel the distinct need to push.

Thankfully, the part about the first egg being the most difficult to birth is true, as the second egg comes out a little easier.

"Rinkon says you are doing well" Lirus calls out.

I respond with a soft grunt, my mind focusing on the fact that I am two eggs down but have five more to go.

I somehow manage to doze off after the fifth egg has left me because fingers are gently caressing my cheek and waking me up.

It takes me a second to realize I'm still in the Birthing Well and that I'm not done.

Nilvone is still sitting in the water in front of me and is speaking softly.

My minute comprehension of Ulian is useless as my brain is unable to make sense of anything at the moment.

"King Nilvone wants you to know that they do not like seeing you in discomfort. Unfortunately the size of the eggs are above average...," Lirus says, her tone sympathetic.

"...You have two eggs still to be birthed. Should you not wish to continue, Rinkon can extract the remaining two but it will lengthen your body's recovery time."

I tilt my head back and gently knock into Zunrion's chest, groaning slightly in frustration.

Hands were running up and down my arms now, doing their best to sooth me.

"There's just two left. I can finish," I say, wincing at the hoarseness of my own voice.

I see Lirus tilt her head in my direction but she's still not looking at me.

She appears concerned.

"You and I, we're built for giving birth to bigger things than this. I'm not going to tap out now."

I do my best to inject a smile into my words, even if it is a tired one, but it has the desired effect as she lets out a quiet chuckle.

I look at Nilvone and then twist to look behind me at Zunrion and try and piece some Ulian together.

"I am fine if you are both here."

They are both quiet, and I think that I may have messed up what I meant to say and begin to ask Lirus.

"Did I—"

My question is cut off as Nilvone's mouth descends onto mine, his lips placing gentle kisses over my lips before his tongue runs over them in a request for entry.

I moan softly into his mouth, my hand moving to cradle his cheek as I reciprocate; my tongue moving to meet his own.

The kiss is slow and lingering, not hurried at all and it's something new that we haven't done before.

The intimacy of it is staggering.

Zunrion is now cupping my breasts, massaging them tenderly and the dual sensation is causing pleasant sparks to shoot through me.

A small cramp higher up in my stomach has us all pausing and much to my embarrassment, I find that Lirus is gone and Rinkon has walked over and is speaking while gesturing towards my stomach.

It takes a bit of charades before I understand that the remaining two eggs haven't dropped into position yet.

Zunrion is gently rubbing my stomach again, trying to get the eggs to move down, but Nilvone is saying something and then there's a bit of a change happening.

Nilvone moves to take Zunrion's place behind me while Zunrion is now kneeling between my legs in front of me.

I look up off to the side at Rinkon, who laughably touches his index finger and thumb together to indicate a circle and then using his other index finger, begins moving it back and forth between his other fingers.

I admit I laugh at the gesture. Sex. Got it.

I worry for a moment about the doctor sticking around but he simply says something professional sounding before leaving the room.

Zunrion's golden honey eyes are gazing at me fondly, and he leans forward to kiss each of my eyelids.

I can feel him willing me to relax through our bond.

It's not a difficult thing for me to do seeing as how I am exhausted.

Kissing begins again in earnest, his lips moving away from my mouth and trailing down my neck where he licks at my skin and nips lightly at the junction between my neck and shoulder.

A moan escapes me just as his hand wanders down between my legs, stroking my folds before his fingers are gone.

As my eyes remain closed, I feel a change in the air around me, his body shifting as close to me as he can get what with my large belly still in the way.

Something is gently prodding me between my legs and I open them wider, the tip of his cock sinking into me.

I giggle as I feel a jet of bubbles where he's inserted himself. Not sure exactly what that is meant to do, I choose to enjoy the unusually pleasant sensation of bubbles tickling my inner folds.

When the bubbling stops, I know this is a chance for me to look down and curiosity makes me do so.

I can't make things out too clearly as the water distorts my view of his lower body, but I catch a glimpse of his cock: a large tendril that is narrow where it's entered me and wider towards his groin. It writhes as if it has a mind of its own, and the movement makes it looks like it shimmering.

There's all sorts of bumps and ridges on it of varying sizes but it is still sleek and shiny and long and-

Oh.

My eyes shut as my head falls back against Nilvone's chest, Zunrion's cock now pushing forward, sliding into me with ease.

My pussy clenches around it as it elongates inside me; no doubt the only reason he's able to sheath himself into me what with my still pregnant stomach in the way.

Like an air pump, I feel his girth expand and just like that, my eyes shoot open again and he's staring at me with such heat that I can't bring myself to look away. His golden honey eyes stay locked on me as he grips my hips underneath the water and thrusts forward; his cock squirming inside me.

A moan slips from my lips as I feel his shaft throb inside me, working its way deeper.

Zunrion leans forward again, catching my mouth with his just as he twitches inside me and something protrudes from his tip, flicking against my cervix as if trying to find a way in.

Tiny pulses are running through me just as I feel a cool slurry of liquid rush in.

Zunrion manages to push himself flush against me; small pumping motions as waves of his hot sap-like cum flood into me. None of it escapes into the water as he's locked in place within me.

My body is quickly overwhelmed as the pressure of his cum against my G-spot is extraordinary.

I buck up into him, my hands grasping his shoulders for balance as I partly dig my nails into his back; the muscles underneath my palms shifting and contracting.

He now changes to a slower pace, fucking me with careful, deliberate thrusts that have me pleading.

"Please, please, faster, I beg you..."

My focus is on trying to impale myself on his dick in an attempt to come.

Zunrion chuckles deeply and fuck me if that doesn't make me almost come right this second.

I hear myself whine as we continue with this lewd dance, moans and pants filling the air around us before he snaps forward harshly and it's enough to take me over the edge.

I lose track of space and time, my whole world narrowing to where Zunrion's touching and pressing into me.

I'm coming with a loud cry, feeling warmth expand out from my core until my fingers and toes are buzzing with it and tears form at the corners of my eyes and threaten to spill over.

Stars explode in my vision before I slump forward, Zunrion still grunting and thrusting into me a few more times before pulling me towards him and holding me to him as much as he is able.

Our chests heave together and we both groan as he slowly slides himself out from within me.

My body is sated and drowsy, and as my head is lolling against Nilvone's chest behind me, there are hands massaging my stomach with those downward strokes and I feel an egg drop within me, already pushing against me.

I don't have any energy to waste on saying anything right now and instead simply grab their offered hands and grip them tight as I begin to push.

Rinkon has appeared again but is remaining quiet as if simply on stand-by.

A familiar flex and release runs through me and I sigh in relief as the egg passes.

One more to go.

Thankfully I feel it already moving down to settle but it feels heavier than the others and I grunt with the sudden pressure.

Something must show in my expression because Rinkon is running that medical device over me.

I look up at him and see him making a shape the size of a grapefruit.

Apparently this seventh and final egg is going to be doozy.

I whimper softly and shake my head.

My strength is gone and I need at least a little recovery time before I can even begin to get this one out but the pressure in me is mounting and my body is telling me to fucking push and push hard.

I cry out as despite my best effort, it's not really budging.

Shutting my eyes tightly, I try and relax, only to pick up on some kind of vibration at the base of my skull.

I have no clue what it is but the more I focus on it the more the vibration picks up and morphs into a pleasant sounding hum which is filling my head like some sort of static.

It clears a moment later.

We are with you.

You are so strong.

We are honored you joined with us.

My eyes shoot open as those thoughts were not my thoughts but they fill me with a burst of energy that has me bearing down one last time.

A satisfied groan leaves me as finally, finally, the last egg comes out.

I feel the briefest of touches against my temple before exhaustion overcomes me and things go dark.

Epilogue: The Bond

Two days later...

I wake up and find Nilvone dozing off in a chair by my bed, his head resting by my side and his hand near mine.

Saying nothing, I watch him for a little while before he must somehow sense I am awake and slowly lifts his head up and looks at me with a small smile.

I smile back, briefly closing my eyes as I feel his hand caress my forehead.

He begins to say something, and clearly he's doing his best to pick simple words in order to speak with me.

The language barrier is getting more and more important for me to overcome each and every day.

Although, maybe it won't matter to them now as I have fulfilled my duty.

I quickly gather that he's trying to ask me if I'm okay, to which I nod.

As I lie here, I attempt to determine whether or not I feel any discomfort at all and realize that there really isn't anything except some lingering tension in my shoulders.

Shifting my legs just little, I don't feel any pain between them either, and my hand my much smaller stomach has me feeling some type of loss now that it's no longer full.

It's still much larger than it should be, but I know it will go down with the next several days.

Nilvone looks relieved that I am feeling well but I sense an aura of uncertainty around him and I begin to get concerned.

"Nilvone?" I question quietly as I lay my hand over his.

For some reason I can't explain I know whatever has him looking this way has nothing to do with the eggs (or well...babies now).

Zunrion appears a moment later and asks me the same question, but now both men are looking at each other and then back at me and my concern is mounting.

They can clearly see from my expression that I am anxious to know what exactly is going on.

Lirus arrives a moment after, and before she can even open her mouth, the kings are speaking in rapid fire Ulian and my head is swiveling between them.

"Will someone just tell me?" I interject now, but not unkindly. Everyone's looking so worked up, myself included.

"They uh—"

My eyes immediately zone in on Lirus, who has never had quite so much trouble finding her words before.

She sees me gripping the sheets around me tightly and realizes she needs to hurry it up.

"Ulian bonding has different…levels…" she throws out there first. "When one chooses life partners here on Ulia, a ceremony formally bonds those together and creates a mental link…"

"Okay…"

"It's like a wedding really, except afterwards you're able to communicate telepathically…"

While fascinating, I'm still not getting it.

"It is extremely rare that such a link is created outside such an event but it appears that…well…I believe you were struggling with the last egg and their majesties' determination to support you somehow caused such a link between you…"

And just like that, I remember.

The humming in my head and then thoughts that weren't my own floating into my mind and helping me see my Nest Day through to the end.

My eyes widen in realization and I look over at Nilvone and Zunrion.

"They did not know that such a link was possible with a human. At least not a link that strong and outside of a unification ceremony" Lirus quickly presses on. "They understand that you will find this to be an invasion of privacy."

"Wait what?"

This was a lot to take in right now and I just wanted to go back to sleep and have the kings smiling over me and not looking at me like they were afraid of my reaction.

I swallow the lump in my throat as I shake my head.

"Does that mean...I can speak with them..." I ask carefully.

Lirus nods.

"They did not wish to presume that you'd be comfortable with the link and so they-"

I close my eyes, half listening to what Lirus is saying now but I can feel that gentle hum in the base of my skull and focus on it.

The humming picks up until it clears away and I do my best to think my words.

Is this working?

Nilvone and Zunrion have different reactions to this.

The former ends up choking on air and the latter has his mouth open in complete shock.

Hello?

There's a gentle push in my mind before voices are speaking clear as day inside of it.

Yes! We hear you...

I can't believe you want to-

Both thoughts tumble into me with warm intent and a laugh escapes me.

Soon afterwards, both men are laughing as well and I'm pretty sure I'm fucking crying too but I don't really care.

Lirus, unbeknownst to me, smiles softly at the three of us before making a graceful exit and leaving the three of us...

Together.

ABOUT THE AUTHOR

A corporate professional by day and an erotica lover by night...(or sometimes during the day as well...)

I am sure I am not the only one who can relate to that sentence!

My erotica sandbox is usually filled with all sorts of breeding, impregnation, and pregnancy kinks...from hot alpha males, shifters, and aliens, to hyper-pregnancies, oviposition (that's all stuff eggs & egg laying in case you don't know ;)), mpreg, and tentacles.

Of course, considering I do have a soft side underneath all the layers of kink and fetish, you will usually see some tender moments peppered in...